Charles A. Underwood

Road Book of Boston and Vicinity

For bicycles, riders, and drivers

Charles A. Underwood

Road Book of Boston and Vicinity
For bicycles, riders, and drivers

ISBN/EAN: 9783337238421

Printed in Europe, USA, Canada, Australia, Japan

Cover: Foto ©Andreas Hilbeck / pixelio.de

More available books at **www.hansebooks.com**

SINGER CYCLES

Weight 27 lbs., less saddle and pedals

The weights of Singer Cycles will invariably be found less than those of machines advertised as light wheels. The lasting properties of Singer wheels are not due to excess of weight.

SINGER & CO.

6 and 8 Berkeley St. and 2 Warren Avenue

BOSTON, MASS.

THE ROAD KING

Fitted with '93 Dunlop Detachable Tires $150.00
Weight 35 lbs.

THE NASSAU

Strictly high grade, the finest balanced and easiest running wheel in the market. Fitted with Phelps & Dingle Tires, $120.00.

THE DUKE

The fastest model yet produced with Goodrich Pneumatic Tires, $100.00.
Send for our complete Bicycle Catalogue, which contains price and style of sundries. Bicycle Shoes and Clothing.

REPAIR WORK

We now have our own shop for all kinds of repair work, including difficult brazing, enameling, nickeling, turning, etc., also **Pneumatic Repair Work of all kinds.** Machines fitted with Pneumatic Tires from $20 to $35, according to kind of tires desired and style of machine. **Correspondence Solicited.**

WRIGHT & DITSON

RETAIL STORE   WHOLESALE
344 Washington Street   95 Pearl Street

BOSTON, MASS.

Have Your Repairing Done

AT THE

L. A. W. Repair Works

1181 & 1182-A Harrison Ave.

BOSTON

Pneumatics and Cushions applied to old wheels
Wheels Built to Order . . . .

⇥ BICYCLES ⇤

BOUGHT
SOLD
AND EXCHANGED

EASY TERMS   CASH OR INSTALMENTS

No Interest Charged

G. A. HUNT

2

A. O. Very Cycle Co.

3

NEW MAIL

36 LBS. LIGHT ROADSTER.

With M. & W. Style, Inner tube Pneumatic Tires, - - -	$125.00
With 1893 model, Dunlop Detachable Pneumatics, - -	135.00
Also New Mail Boy's Diamond Frame Safety, Handsomest Boy's Wheel made, - - - - - - - -	60.00
Also our Cheap Line of Wheels, $15 to $85, Best in Market.	

DESCRIPTION.

Credenda Tubing ; long 10 inch Ball Head ; Single butt ended spokes, laced and strongly tied at intersections ; lapped Rim very stiff ; NEW MAIL low Handle Bars; Cork handles ; 3-8 in. best Chain ; 6 1-2 in. round steel forged Cranks; Dust proof Ball Pedals with Square rubbers ; Garford Saddle ; Tools complete ; Weight stripped 36 lbs. 60 in. gear. 28 in. rear and 30 front wheel.

A HIGH GRADE SAFETY.

MANUFACTURERS,

WM. READ & SONS,

107 Washington Street, - - Boston.

4

ROAD BOOK

OF

BOSTON

AND

VICINITY

FOR

Bicyclers, Riders and Drivers

EDITED BY

CHARLES A. UNDERWOOD

L.A.W. Consul for Jamaica Plain

SEVENTH EDITION

Copyright 1893, by Road Book of Boston Co

BOSTON
THE SPAKELL PRINT
1893

5

There and back!

You'll go Faster, Safer and Easier on
a VICTOR than on any
other bicycle

VICTOR FLYER—29 Pounds

Come in and let us show you why
VICTORS are the Best for you

Overman Wheel Co.

Boston Branch==182 Columbus Ave.

Catalogue Free

Index to Places and Distances
from Boston

9

It depends

on where you live, whether we can be of any use to you, but if you are thinking of getting a **Victor, Columbia, Union, Lovell Diamond, Hickory, Keating or McCune** and you have a Second-Hand Wheel to turn in as part payment or you wish to buy on Easy Payments, better come and see us. We can do you good. . . . .

J. M. Linscott & Co.

MALDEN STORE
Eastern Ave. and Ferry St.

CHELSEA STORE
Broadway and 3d St

13

COPLEY SQUARE, WHERE ALL ROUTES IN THIS BOOK BEGIN

ROUTE ONE.

To Chestnut Hill Reservoir
via Beacon St., or Commonwealth Ave.

Copley square

	Dartmouth street	Excellent
Left	Commonwealth avenue	"
Through	Back Bay Park	
Left	Beacon street	"
	Chestnut Hill Reservoir	5 miles

    Beacon street is the shortest route to the Reservoir, is the finest boulevard in the country, and the delight and pride of wheelmen. Commonwealth avenue leads direct to the main entrance and has no superior as a good road and abounds in some fine coasts.

ROUTE TWO.

Chestnut Hill Reservoir to Boston
via Brookline and Longwood.

Main Entrance.

	Commonwealth avenue		Excellent
Right	Washington street		Good
Left	Park street		"
Right	Marion street (Coast.) }	Brook-	Excellent
Left	Harvard street	line.	"
Right	Sewall avenue		"
Left	Kent street		"
Right	Dudley street	Long-	"
Left	Hawes street	wood.	"
Right	Monmouth street		"
Left	St. Mary's street		"
Right	Beacon street		"
Right	Dartmouth street		"
	Copley Square		5 miles

    This is one of the finest and most popular routes about Boston, its many turnings lead one through cool and shady avenues, lined by many of the finest suburban residences. It is a favorite return route for Reservoir moonlight parties.

18

ROUTE THREE.

To Chestnut Hill Reservoir via Franklin Park.

	Copley square	
	Dartmouth street	Excellent
Right	Columbus avenue	Asphalt
Left	West Chester Park	Excellent
Right	Harrison avenue	Good
Left	Warren street	"
Right	Walnut avenue	Excellent
	FRANKLIN PARK	
Right	Glen Road. (Coast.)	Good
	Green street	
	JAMAICA PLAIN	4 miles
Left	Centre street	Excellent
Right	May street	"
Left	Pond street	"
Right	Newton street	"
Right	Hammond street	"
Right	Beacon street. (Coast.)	"
	Rear Entrance.	9¾ miles

The Reservoir Drive is exceedingly popular among cyclists, who generally congregate at the watering-trough, at the lower basin. It was at this place that G. R. Aggassiz won the championship mile, in 3.21½; and R. S. Codman made the quarter-mile record for the country, in 38 5-8 seconds, at the Suffolk Bicycle Club races in the early days of cycling. The Drive of the lower basin measures 1 16 (1.17) miles in the middle of the way, with the scratch at the watering-trough.

ROUTE FOUR.

Harvard Square to Belmont Springs.

	Harvard square	
Left	Brattle street	Good
	MOUNT AUBURN.	1 1-2 miles
Right	Belmont street	Good
Right	Lexington street	"
	WAVERLY.	4 1-2 miles
Cross	Railroad.	
Right	Mill street	
Left	Water street	
	BELMONT SPRINGS.	6 1-2 miles

ROUTE FIVE.

To Cambridgeport, via Cottage Farm.

	Copley square	
	Dartmouth street	Excellent
Left	Commonwealth avenue	"
	Cottage Farm Bridge	"
Right	Essex Street Bridge	"
	Brookline street	"
Left	Chestnut street	"
Right	Magazine street	"
	Central square	3 1-4 miles

ROUTE SIX.

Park Route.

	Copley square	
	Boylston street	Excellent
Through	Back Bay Park	"
Left	Beacon street	"
Right	Chestnut Hill avenue	"
	Chestnut Hill Reservoir	"
	Main Entrance	
Right	Beacon street	"
Left	Hammond street	"
Left	Newton street	"
	Pond street	"
	Coast Carefully	
Right	May street	Good
Left	Centre street	"
	Arnold Arboretum	
Left	South street	"
	Forest Hills Station	
Cross	Railroad	
	Morton street	"
Left	Ellicott street	"
Right	Walnut avenue	"
	FRANKLIN PARK	

The Driveway around Franklin Park is 200 feet less than a mile. Return by reverse of route 3.

ROUTE SEVEN.

To Riverside.

	Copley square	
	Dartmouth street	
Left	Commonwealth avenue	Excellent
Left	Beacon street	"
Right	Chestnut Hill avenue	"
	BRIGHTON	4 miles
	Washington street to	
	Oak square	Excellent
Left	Tremont street	"
Right	Park street	"
Left	NEWTON	6 miles
Cross	Rail Road	
Left	Washington street	Good
	NEWTONVILLE	7 3-4 miles
	WEST NEWTON	8 3-4 miles
Right	Woodland avenue	
	AUBURNDALE	9 miles
Left	Auburn street	
	Charles street	
	RIVERSIDE	10 miles

Fine place for boating. Boats to let. Newton Boat Club House is located here. Dinner can be obtained at the house of Mr. Edward Anderson, favorite rendezvous of Roxbury Club.

ROUTE EIGHT.

To Gloucester via Essex.

Same as route thirty-nine to Ipswich		35 3-4 miles
Right	Essex street	Excellent
Right	Northern avenue	"
	ESSEX	40 1-4 miles
Right	Southern avenue	Excellent
Through	Essex woods	
Left	School street	Excellent
	MANCHESTER	44 3-4 miles
Left	Summer street	Excellent
Left	Western avenue	"
	GLOUCESTER	52 miles

The road from Ipswich to Manchester is one of the finest in the state, and the ride through Essex woods is beautiful.

Sidwell & Saben Cycle Co.

243 Columbus Avenue, Boston.

SOLE MANUFACTURERS OF

S. & S.

CYCLES

ALSO NEW ENGLAND AGENTS FOR THE

QUINTON SCORCHER

To Corey Hill.

Copley square

	Dartmouth street	Excellent
Left	Commonwealth avenue	Good
Left	St. Paul street	''
Right	Longwood avenue	''
Right	Harvard avenue	''
Left	Beacon street	''
Right	Summit Hill avenue	''
	Corey Hill	3 miles

Corey Hill was first overcome by Mr. H. D. Corey, of Boston and at that time was considered insurmountable, but since then has been ridden by both bicycles and tricycles.

Length of Corey Hill, 2,300 feet; height, 199 feet; average rise, 1 foot in 11.41; steepest grade, last 158 feet, 1 foot in 7.85.

The view from the top of the hill well repays for the labor of ascending it, on foot if necessary. The last 159 feet is what generally bowls over the cyclists.

The route can be shortened by going straight out Beacon street to Summit Hill avenue.

ROUTE TEN.

To Harvard Square.

Copley square, Dartmouth street, left, Newbury street, right, W. Chester Park, over Harvard Bridge, Main street, (Cambridge,) Harvard Square 4 miles; excellent roads all the way.

Harvard University joins Harvard square. Cyclists should especially inspect Hemenway Gymnasium, Memorial Hall, Agassiz Museum and the Washington Elm, on the north side of the Square. Holmes' field has a one-half mile Bicycle Track.

The Novelty Cyclometer

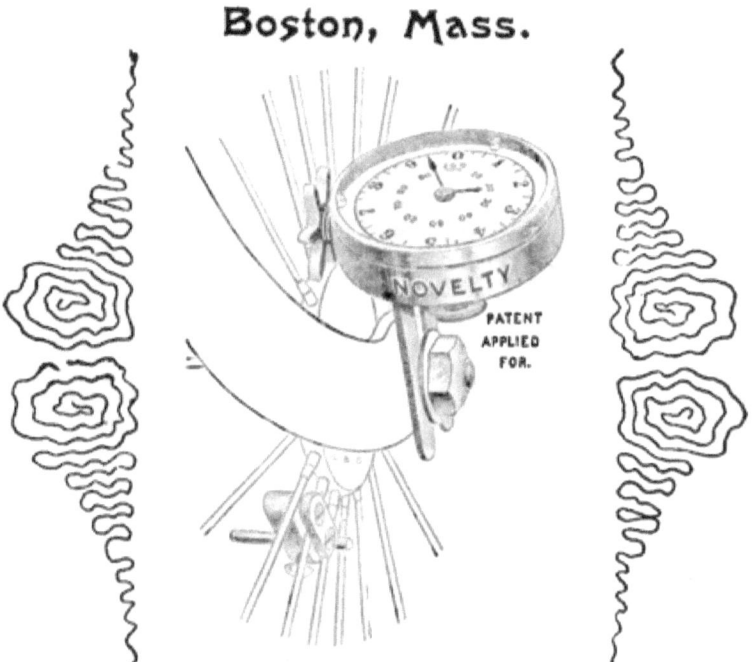

Has all desirable features, being light, simple, accurate, easily read from the saddle, and readily attached to the front fork of the bicycle.

Runs to one hundred miles and repeats, or can be set at zero, for each ride and with the accompanying water-proof record book, the number of miles ridden and places visited, each day, or trip, may be retained for ready reference.

Made for all Sizes of Wheels
PRICE, $5.00

ROUTE ELEVEN.

To Franklin Park, Forest Hills, and Mt. Hope Cemeteries.

	Copley square	
	Dartmouth street	Good
Right	Columbus avenue	Asphalt
Left	W. Chester Park	Excellent
Right	Harrison avenue	Good
Left	Warren street	"
Right	Walnut avenue	Excellent
	FRANKLIN PARK	
Right	Morton street	Good
	FOREST HILLS CEMETERY	
Left	Walkhill street	"
	MOUNT HOPE CEMETERY	

In passing out of Franklin Park go through gates at right of the overlook, follow this avenue to Morton street to Washington street, then turn sharp to the left to Walkhill street. Forest Hills Cemetery ranks second to Mount Auburn, and like it, is owned by a private corporation. Mt. Hope belongs to the city. Mt. Calvary Cemetery (Catholic) adjoins Mt. Hope. Bicycles are not allowed in any of the cemeteries.

ROUTE TWELVE.

To Brockton.

Copley square, Dartmouth street, good, Right, Columbus avenue, asphalt, left, Chester Park, excellent, right, Boston street, good, left, Hancock street, good, Left, Adams street, excellent, MILTON LOWER MILLS, 6 1-2 miles, EAST MILTON, 8 1-2 miles, QUINCY, 11 miles right. Hancock street, right, School street, left, Franklin street, Independent avenue, and Washington street, are good, SOUTH BRAINTREE, 14 1-2 miles, HOLBROOK, 18 miles, Franklin street, right Howard street, left Main street, are good, BROCKTON, 23 miles.

ROUTE THIRTEEN,

To Pumping Station.

Copley square

Left	Dartmouth street	Excellent
Right	Columbus avenue	Asphalt
Left	Chester Park	Excellent
Left	Swett street	,,
Right	Boston street	,,
Left	Cottage street	,,
Cross	Dorchester avenue	,,
	Crescent avenue	,,
Left	Carson street	Good
Cross	Old Colony R. R.	
	Mt. Vernon street	Excellent.
	PUMPING STATION	4 miles

This is a favorite evening run. The station is located in what is called the Cow Pasture, Dorchester Bay, and from the end of the pier, which is nearly a mile from land, a fine view of the harbor can be obtained. Riders should visit the buildings, as some of the largest pumps in the country are located here, pumping the waste water from the city into the tunnel, which conveys it nearly two miles under the bay to Moon Island, where it empties into the ocean. This run will prove both pleasant and instructive.

ROUTE FOURTEEN.

To Union Market House.

Copley square

	Dartmouth street			Excellent
Left	Commonwealth avenue	}	Mile	,,
Right	Brighton avenue	}	Ground	,,
Right	North Beacon street			,,
	Charles River Bridge			
	United States Arsenal			
Right	Walnut street			,,
Left	Union Market House			5 1-4 miles

The Union House can be telephoned from Boston. The hotel is much patronized by Cattle dealers, and its substantial cuisine, particularly steaks and other meats has earned a well deserved reputation among the always hungry cyclists.

BICYCLES - 60 Sudbury St. - BICYCLES

JOHN WOOD, JR.

Columbia & Lovell Diamond

BICYCLES.

Agent for Pope Mfg. Co. 13 years.

71 to 77 Rantoul St.,	60 Sudbury Street,
BEVERLY, MASS.	BOSTON, MASS.

BICYCLES - 60 Sudbury St. - BICYCLES

ROUTE FIFTEEN.

To Somerville.

	Copley square	
	Dartmouth street	Excellent ·
Left	Newbury street	"
Right	W. Chester Park	"
Over	Harvard Bridge	"
	Main street ⎫	"
	CAMBRIDGE to ⎬	3 miles
	Central square ⎪	
	CAMBRIDGEPORT ⎭	
Right	Prospect street	Excellent
Left	Webster avenue	"
	Union square ⎫	4 1-2 miles
	SOMERVILLE ⎭	

On Central Hill (via Summer street, Right, Walnut street, left, Highland avenue,) is located the old fort, constructed partially of Revolutionary relics. The view from the hill embraces the adjoining towns for miles around.

ROUTE SIXTEEN.

To Mt. Auburn.

	Copley square	
	Dartmouth street	Excellent
Left	Newbury street	"
Right	W. Chester Park	"
Over	Harvard Bridge	"
	Main street ⎫	"
	CAMBRIDGE ⎭	
	Harvard square	4 miles
	Brattle street	
	MOUNT AUBURN	5 1-4 miles

Mt. Auburn was established by the Massachusetts Horticultural Society in 1831, and is the oldest garden cemetery in America. Its horticultural beauties are upon the grandest scale.

For Fresh Pond take Fresh Pond Lane opposite Mt. Auburn.

SWIFT by nature

SWIFT by name

Weight 32 lbs. complete

115,000 in use

COVENTRY MACHINISTS CO.   239 Columbus Ave., BOSTON

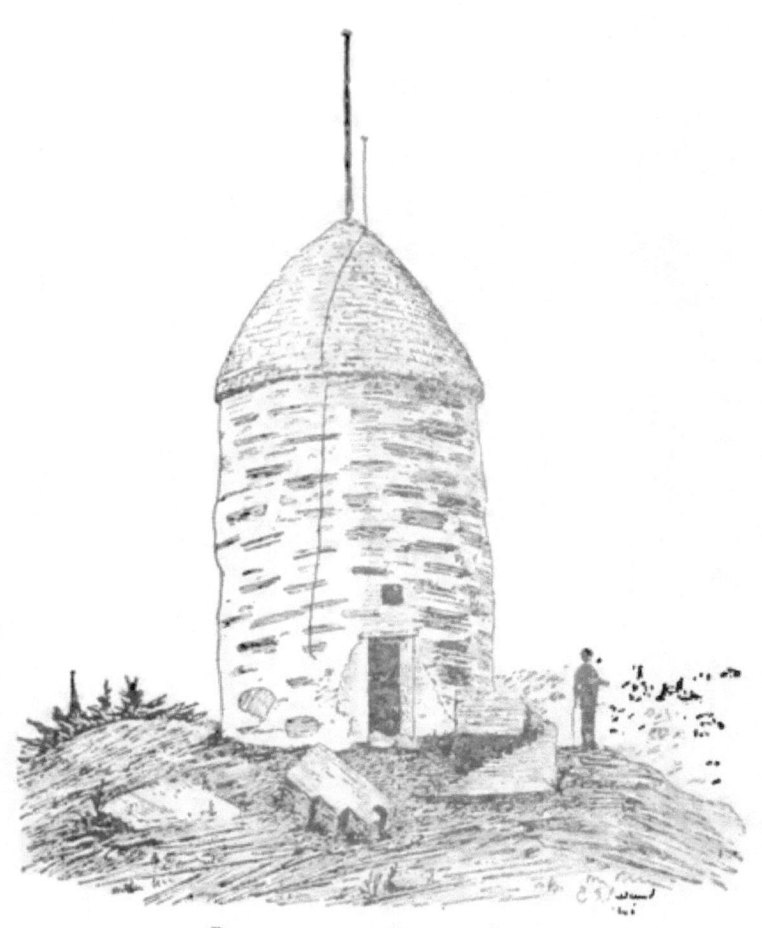

BUILT ABOUT 1703

OLD POWDER HOUSE, SOMERVILLE
All routes to Lynn pass this house.

The Powder House, or old mill, has few rivals in the country in historical interest. The exact date when it was built is not known. It was originally a grist mill, and was probably built by John Mallett, who came into possession of the site in 1703-4. In his will, made in 1720, "the grist mill" is left to his two sons. The mill was undoubtedly built several years previous to 1720, and for some time after that it continued to grind the corn for the farmers for many miles around.

The powder House commemorates one of the earliest hostilities of the revolution. On the morning of Sept. 1, 1774, Gen. Gage sent an expedition to seize the powder at the magazine, and 260 soldiers embarked at Long wharf, in Boston and proceeded up Mystic river, landing at Ten Hills farm, from whence they marched to the Powder House. The 250 half-barrels of powder which the magazine contained were speedily transferred to the boats and removed to Castle William (now Fort Independence) in Boston harbor.

ROUTE SEVENTEEN.

Middlesex Fells and Spot Pond.

	Copley square	
	Dartmouth street	Excellent
Left	Newbury street	"
Right	W. Chester Park	"
Over	Harvard Bridge	"
	Main street } Cambridge }	4 miles
Cross	Harvard square	
	North avenue	Excellent
	Porter's Station	5 1-4 miles
Right	Russell street	
Left	Elm street	
Cross	Broadway	
	Harvard street	
Left	College avenue	Good
Right	Pearl street	"
Left	Medford street	"
	Medford	8 miles
Left	Forest street	Good
	Middlesex Fells } Spot Pond }	10 miles

A favorite resort for cycle picnics, and for participants in Sunday runs. There is no good hotel near by. Boats can be hired for rowing and sailing. The roads near the pond are quite hilly.

ROUTE EIGHTEEN.

To Mt. Wauchusett, Princeton.

Same as Route Twenty-three to Northboro.

Northboro, 34 miles, South Berlin, 36 1-2 miles Berlin, 38 1-2 miles, West Berlin, 40 miles, Clinton, 42 1-2 miles, Sterling, 48 miles, East Princeton, 53 miles, Mount Wauchusett, 56 miles.

The roads beyond Clinton are from good to bad. The hills should all be coasted carefully.

ROUTE NINETEEN.

Around Great Sign Boards.

	Copley square	
	Dartmouth street	Excellent
Left	Newbury street	"
Left	Cambridge street	"
	BRIGHTON	4 1-2 miles
	Washington street	Good
	NEWTON	6 3-4 miles
	NEWTONVILLE	7 3-4 miles
	WEST NEWTON	8 3-4 miles
	GREAT SIGN BOARDS	10 1-2 miles
Left	Beacon street	Excellent
	CHESTNUT HILL RESERVOIR	15 miles

Return from Reservoir by Reverse of Route No. 2.

This Route stands second in favor of Boston wheelmen, and is especially utilized for moonlight and short club runs. The return into the Reservoir is a trifle hilly, but the road bed is of the best, and the route includes many of the numerous superb country seats about Boston.

ROUTE TWENTY.

To Hunnewell Estate.

	Copley square	
	Dartmouth street	Excellent
Left	Commonwealth avenue	"
Left	Beacon street	"
Pass	Chestnut Hill Reservoir	
	Great Sign Boards	
	NEWTON LOWER FALLS	10 miles
	WELLESLEY HILLS	11 1-2 miles
	WELLESLEY	13 1-4 miles
Left	Washington street	Good
	HUNNEWELL ESTATE	14 1-2 miles

The Hunnewell Estate is private, but the public is generally allowed access to the grounds, through the courtesy of Mr. Hunnewell, upon application at the mansion. The gardens are beautifully laid out after the old English style, and overlook Lake Wauban and Wellesley College.

ECHO BRIDGE

ROUTE TWENTY-ONE

To Echo Bridge, Newton.

	Copley square	
	Dartmouth street	Excellent
Left	Commonwealth avenue	"
Left	Beacon street	"
	Chestnut Hill Reservoir	5 miles
	NEWTON CENTRE	7 miles
Left	Centre street	Excellent
	NEWTON HIGHLANDS	8 1-4 miles
Right	Boylston street	Excellent
Left	ECHO BRIDGE	9 1-4 miles

Echo Bridge is a granite span over the Charles River, and supports the Conduit of the Boston Water Works. Nine distinct echoes can be heard from the blast of the bugle.

ROUTE TWENTY-TWO.

To Lexington via Arlington.

	Copley square	
	Dartmouth street	Excellent
Left	Newbury street	"
Right	W. Chester Park	"
Over	Harvard Bridge	"
	Main street, CAMBRIDGE	"
Cross	Harvard square	4 miles
	North avenue	Good
	PORTER'S STATION	5 1-4 miles
	ARLINGTON	7 miles
	Arlington avenue	Poor
	EAST LEXINGTON	10 miles
	LEXINGTON (Common)	12 1-4 miles
	Lexington Monument	

Return via reverse of Route 24.

This route from North avenue and beyond is substantially the path taken by the British troops on the way to the Battles of Lexington and Concord, and along the road are many mementos of those Revolutionary events. Route 24 gives much better wheeling but is devoid of historical points of interest.

WHITNEY HOUSE

WESTBORO, MASS.

L. A. W. HOTEL

32 MILES FROM BOSTON.

GOOD ROADS, THROUGH A DELIGHTFUL COUNTRY
ALL THE WAY.

$2.00 per Day. = Dinner, 50 cts.

BEST HOTEL BETWEEN BOSTON AND WORCESTER
STEAM HEAT, ELECTRIC LIGHTS AND BELLS
FIRST CLASS IN EVERY PARTICULAR

Special Attention to the Comfort and Accommo=
dation of Wheelmen.

FRANK H. MARTIN, - - PROP.

ROUTE TWENTY-THREE.

To Worcester.

Copley square

	Dartmouth street	Excellent
Left	Commonwealth avenue	"
Left	Beacon street	"
Pass	Reservoir	"
	Beacon street	"
	NEWTON CENTRE	7 miles
	Beacon street	Excellent
	NEWTON LOWER FALLS	
	WELLESLEY HILLS	11 1-2 miles
	WELLESLEY	13 1-4 miles
	NATICK	17 1-4 miles

At Natick Common turn to the left and take first on the right (Pond street) to Mill street, which leads back to the Main road again and thus avoid the sand along the west shore of Cochituate Lake.

SOUTH FRAMINGHAM, 20 miles, Cross, B. & A. A. R. R. to the right, Concord street, Good, left, Union avenue Good, FRAMINGHAM CENTRE, 22 miles, Cross, O. C. R. R. Around Reservoir, Under Railroad Bridge, SOUTHBORO', 29 miles, NORTHBORO', 34 miles, SHREWSBURY, 40 miles, WORCESTER, 45 miles.

At Framingham Reservoir the " sand paper " district practically ends. The roads to Southboro' are good; beyond there fair, but an old rider may ride from Boston to Worcester without a dismount. The Deerfoot Farms and St. Marks School are located in Southboro'.

At Framingham Centre take road indicated by Sign Board marked Worcester. One mile west of Southboro' take right hand road for Worcester and left hand for Westboro' (3 miles.) At Shrewsbury take new road to Worcester. For Marlboro' (4 miles) take right hand road at Southboro'.

37

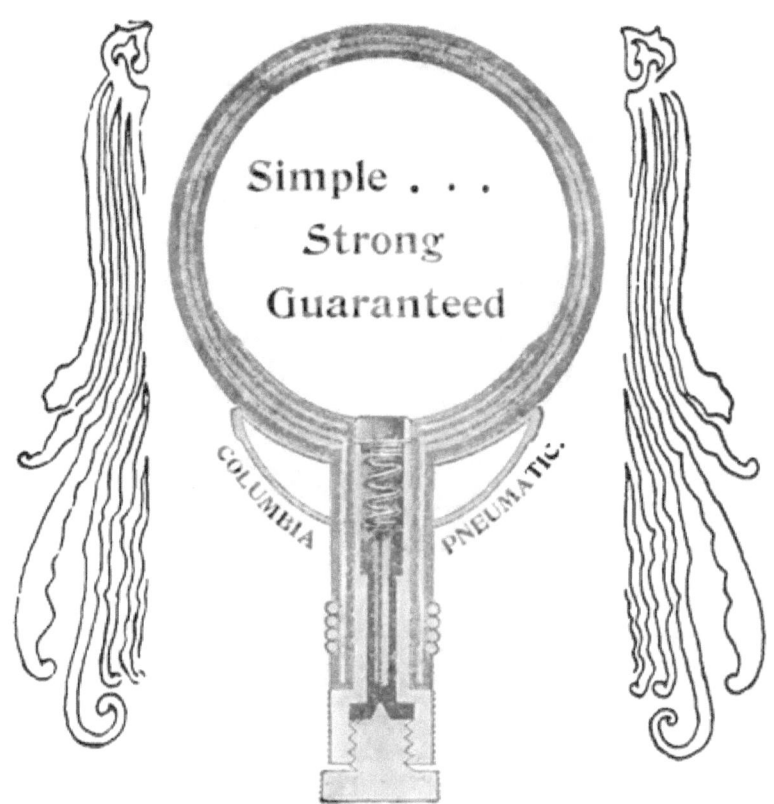

Simple . . .
Strong
Guaranteed

COLUMBIA PNEUMATIC.

"United We Stand"

The COLUMBIA has its inner tube "united" to outer cover and thus "stands" under COLUMBIA riders.

No walking home when you use a COLUMBIA.

Pope Mfg. Co.

Boston   New York   Chicago   Hartford

To Lexington via Waverly.

Copley square.

	Dartmouth street	Excellent
Left	Commonwealth avenue) Mile	"
Left	Brighton avenue } Ground	"
Right	Linden street	"
Right	Cambridge street	"
Left	North Harvard street	"
	Brighton street	"
Left	Mt. Auburn street	Good
	MT. AUBURN	5 3-4 miles
	Belmont street	Fair
Right	North street	"
	WAVERLY	8 1-2 miles
	EAST LEXINGTON	11 1-2 miles
Left	Main road	Fair
	LEXINGTON	13 1-2 miles

This route is about a mile longer than No. 22. The road bed is excellent, and it is recommended to those who prefer good riding to viewing historical landscapes.

ROUTE TWENTY-FIVE.

Milton Lower Mills to West and South Quincy.

MILTON LOWER MILLS. Adams street. Milton Hill. EAST MILTON STATION, 1 1-2 miles. RAILWAY VILLAGE, 2 miles. Right, Common street, good. WEST QUINCY, 3 1-2 miles. Left, Water street, fair. Right, Franklin street, fair. SOUTH QUINCY, 5 miles.

At the foot of Franklin street hill are located two old fashioned houses, the birthplaces of John Adams and John Quincy Adams. From the top of Penn's Hill, close by, Mrs. John Adams and young Quincy Adams watched the Battle of Bunker Hill, and saw the departure of the British fleet from Boston. Scattered through the township of Quincy are many other historical points of interest pertaining to Revolutionary times, directly connected with the Adams and Hancock families.

The Acknowledged Standard

The best and most favorably known

The most completely guaranteed

The result of fifteen years of experience in manufacture

The wheel that holds world's records
The favorite

The **COLUMBIA**

Pope Mfg. Co.

221 Columbus Ave., - - Boston.

Boston to Concord and Acton.

Copley square

	Dartmouth street	Excellent
Left	Newbury street	"
Right	West Chester Park	"
Over	Harvard Bridge	
	Main street, CAMBRIDGE	
Cross	Harvard square	4 miles
	PORTER'S STATION	5 1-4 miles
	ARLINGTON	7 miles
	Arlington avenue	Good
	EAST LEXINGTON	10 miles
	LEXINGTON (Common.)	12 1-4 miles
	Monument street	Poor
	Lexington Road	"
	CONCORD (Common)	18 miles
	Main street	
	CONCORD JUNC.	20 miles
	Laws Brook Road to So. Acton	23 miles

About one mile this side of the Common is the old Nathaniel Hawthorne house (with tower,) with Hawthorne's walk between it and the Alcott house, and the chapel of the Concord School of Philosophy adjoining. A half-mile further on, in the forks of the road, is the Emerson homestead. Just at the entrance to the village on the left is the old Wright Tavern. On the right, down Monument street, are the Old Manse and "One Arch Bridge," the scene of the Battle of Concord. On Main street are the Concord Library and the old Thoreau house, the present home of A. Bronson and Louise M. Alcott. In the old Court house is the C. E. Davis collection of relics. The first Provincial Congress was held in the Unitarian Church edifice, near the Wright Tavern.

Massapoag Lake Hotel, Sharon, Mass.

Open from May to October. 18 miles from Boston on Providence Division Old Colony Railroad. Beautifully situated on the banks of one of the largest lakes in Massachusetts. Good roads. Excellent cuisine. A beautiful new steamer. Special attention to the comforts of bicyclists.

A. Park Boyce & Co., Proprietors.

Telephone Connections.

ROUTE TWENTY-SEVEN.

To Massapoag House, Sharon.

	Copley square	
	Dartmouth street	Good
Right	Columbus avenue	Asphalt
Left	W. Chester Park	Excellent
Right	Harrison avenue	Good
Left	Warren street	"
Right	Walnut avenue	Excellent
	FRANKLIN PARK	4 miles
Right	Through Gates to	
Right	Morton street	Good
	Austin street	"
Right	Blue Hill avenue	"
	MATTAPAN	7 miles
	BLUE HILL	
	Washington street	Good
	PONKAPOAG	
	CANTON	13 miles
	SHARON	18 miles
	MASSAPOAG LAKE HOTEL	

Another Route is from Copley square, Columbus
avenue, Chester Park, Harrison avenue, Warren street,
Blue Hill avenue, past Mattapan station, New York and
New England Railroad, straight out past the west side
of Blue Hill, through Ponkapoag Village, then bear to
the right, pass the cemeteries, South Canton, pass the
station Stoughton Branch Railroad, Cobb's Tavern,
Massapoag Lake, to the Massapoag Lake Hotel — 18 1-2
miles.

Driving distances from the hotel to adjacent towns,
Moose Hill, 4 miles,; Canton, 5 miles; Stoughton, Wal-
pole, and Foxboro, 6 miles; Brockton, 12 miles; Norwood,
10 miles; Dedham 14 miles.

To South Natick via Needham. Same as Route Forty-three to

	WEST ROXBURY	7 miles
Cross	Charles River Bridge	
Right	Needham street	
	Causeway street	Excellent
	Great Plain avenue	"
	NEEDHAM	11 1-2 miles
	WELLESLEY	15 1-2 miles
	SOUTH NATICK	17 3-4 miles

The roads by this route are especially fine. Great
Plain avenue in Needham has no superior as a road bed.

43

We Were Born

of poor **BUT** honest

parents

consequently

We can appreciate the position of the man who wants a wheel and has not the ready cash to pay for it. We have all the leading makes and sell them on terms to suit. We rent, repair, exchange and sell on commission.

Boston Cycle Exchange

660 Centre Street.

All Jamaica Plain Cars pass the Door

ROUTE TWENTY-EIGHT.

To Concord via Waltham.

Copley square, **Dartmouth** street, Excellent, left, Commonwealth avenue, and Right, Brighton avenue, (mile ground) excellent, right, North Beacon street, excellent, WATERTOWN, 5 3-4 miles, Main street, Good, **Waltham, 8 3-4** miles, **Main street, good,** Cross, Mass. **Central R. R.,** Right, **Weston Station, 12** 1-4 miles, **Left,** North avenue, Fair, **Cross,** Fitchburg R. R. **Right, Fork of Roads,** Fair, SOUTH LINCOLN, Right, **Walden street, Fair,** Walden Pond, CONCORD, 18 3-4 mile.

ROUTE TWENTY-NINE.

To Woodlawn Park Hotel via Newton.

Copley square

	Dartmouth street	Excellent
Left	Commonwealth avenue) Mile	"
Right	Brighton avenue) Ground	"
Left	Cambridge street	"
	BRIGHTON	
	Washington street	Good
	NEWTON	6 3-4 miles
	NEWTONVILLE	7 3-4 miles
	WEST NEWTON	8 3-4 miles
	Washington street	Good
	Woodlawn Park Hotel	9 1-2 miles

Return via "Great Sign Boards" and Beacon street to Chestnut Hill Reservoir, as given in Route 2 and 19. It is the rule for wheelmen to dine at the Woodland Park Hotel, when in the vicinity, and it is seldom that during the riding season one cannot find wheelmen there.

To Essex House, Salem.

	Copley square	
	Boylston street	Excellent
Right	W. Chester Park	"
Over	Harvard Bridge	"
	Main street, CAMBRIDGE	
Cross	Harvard square	3 miles
Left	North avenue	Excellent
Right	Day street	
	Railroad station	
Left	Cross track	
	Elm street	
	Old Powder House	
	College avenue	
Right	George street	
Left	Main street	
	Medford square	7 1-2 miles

Salem street, City square, Malden, 9 1-2 miles, right, Main street, left, Eastern avenue, Broadway, Maplewood, 11 miles, left, Broadway, Salem street, watering trough, East Saugus, 14 3-4 miles, left, Boston street, Tower Hill, left, Common street, Lynn Common, 16 3-4 miles, Common street, left, Essex street, Lafayette street, cross bridge, Central street, right, ESSEX HOUSE, 22 3-4 miles.

At Malden pump take Ferry street, left, Elm street, for Woodlawn Cemetery

This is one of the favorite runs of Boston wheelmen and one is always likely to find wheelmen at dinner at the Essex House. This route can be somewhat shortened by taking the Chelsea Ferry, between Boston and Chelsea (See last part of Route 57.)

An excellent after-dinner trip can be made by crossing the bridge into Beverly, and on to Manchester and Gloucester, following the shore road. For points of interest in and about Gloucester read, "In and around Cape Ann." by J. S. Webber, Jr. of Gloucester.

Dame, Stoddard & Kendall

NEW ENGLAND AGENTS FOR

The Eagle Altair

No. 1 Road Wheel, weight 30 lbs.

No. 2 Road Wheel, weight 30 lbs.

No. 3 Track Racer, Aluminum Rims, 20 lbs.

No. 4 Road Racer, Aluminum Rims, 24 lbs

CALL AND EXAMINE

DAME, STODDARD & KENDALL

374 Washington and
2 Franklin Streets

· · · · · · · BOSTON · · · · · · ·

ROUTE THIRTY-ONE.

To Charlestown, Everett. Malden, Melrose, Wakefield, Reading, No. Reading, Andover and Lawrence.

	Copley square	
	Dartmouth street	Excellent
Right	Beacon street	"
Left	Temple street	
Through	Stamford street	Pavements
	Causeway street to	"
	Warren avenue	"
	City square CHARLESTOWN	2 miles
Left	Bow street	Good
Left	Rutherford avenue	"
	Sullivan square	3 1-4 miles
Right	Oxford street over Malden Bridge to	
	EVERETT STATION	5 1-4 miles

Left, Main street, MALDEN, 7 miles, MELROSE, 9 miles, MELROSE HIGHLANDS 10 1-4 miles, WAKEFIELD, 12 3-4 miles, READING, 15 3-4 miles, ANDOVER, 25 1-4 miles, LAWRENCE 29 1-2 miles.

ROUTE THIRTY-TWO.

To Woodlawn Park Hotel. via Great Sign Boards.

	Copley square	
	Dartmouth street	Excellent
Left	Commonwealth avenue	"
Left	Beacon street	"
To	Great Sign Boards	
Right	Washington street	"
	WOODLAWN PARK HOTEL	

Return by reverse of Route 19.

NANTASKET BEACH

To Nantasket Beach, Hull, and Downer's Landing.

Copley square

	Dartmouth street	Good
Right	Columbus avenue	Asphalt
Left	Chester Park	Excellent
Right	Harrison avenue	Good
Left	Warren street	"
Left	Washington street	"
	Codman Hill	
	Milton Hill	
	Adams street	Excellent
	EAST MILTON	8 miles
	QUINCY	10 1-2 miles
	Washington street	Good
	QUINCY POINT	12 1-4 miles
	NORTH WEYMOUTH	14 miles
	Bridge street	Fair
	Lincoln street	"
	HINGHAM	17 miles
	Rockland street	Fair
	NANTASKET P. O.	19 1-2 miles
	HULL	24 miles

At Nantasket P. O. take Jerusalem Road to the right for shore hotels and restaurants in Cohasset; and to the left for Nantasket Beach resorts. The roads in the vicinity of the beach are more or less sandy, particularly so in dry weather.

For Downer's Landing take the first left-hand road after passing Weymouth Draw Bridge.

Downer's Landing is a seashore summer resort in Boston Harbor, and its clam and fish dinners are popular with cyclists.

The return to Boston can be made by cars or steamer.

PRINTING
BINDING

DESIGNING
ENGRAVING

55 Franklin Street, Boston

To Franklin Park and Return.

Copley square

	Dartmouth street	Good
Right	Columbus avenue	Asphalt
Left	Chester Park	Excellent
Right	Harrison avenue	Good
Left	Warren street	"
Right	Walnut avenue	Excellent
	FRANKLIN PARK	3 3-4 miles

The land occupied by Franklin Park covers about 500 acres more or less of fields and woodlands and is fast approaching completion. There are miles of the finest of macadamized roads completed in the park and the drive around the play ground is the pride of Boston wheelmen. The city Fourth of July races are run here. The wheelmen congregate at the spring at the lower end of the playground. Going toward Morton street there is a fine coast of a half mile. On any pleasant Sunday hundreds of wheels may be seen here.

Right	Morton street	
Cross	Old Colony R. R.	
Left	South street	Good
Through	Arnold Aboretum	
Right	Centre street	Fine Coast
Left	May street	Excellent
Right	Pond street	"
Left	Prince street	"
Right	Perkins street (Jamaica Pond.)	
Left	Chestnut street	Sharp Coast
Right	Sewall street	Excellent
	Cypress street	"
	School street	"
	Aspinwall avenue	"
	St. Paul street	"
Right	Beacon street	"
Right	Dartmouth street	"
	Copley square	

(Cypress street, School street, Aspinwall avenue, St. Paul street — Brook-line.)

This route although containing many turns, leads through fine streets, mostly macadamized. Starting in Boston, out through Roxbury, Jamaica Plain, Brookline, the distance is about ten miles, and can be easily covered in two hours.

ROUTE THIRTY-FIVE.

To Charlestown, Bunker Hill, and Navy Yard.

	Copley square	
	Dartmouth street	Excellent
Left	Newbury street	"
Right	Chester Park	"
Over	Harvard Bridge	"
	Main street, CAMBRIDGE	"
	Central square	2 miles
Right	Prospect street	Excellent
Left	Washington street	Good
	Sullivan square } CHARLESTOWN }	4 1-2 miles
Right	Rutherford street	Good
Left	Austin street	"
Cross	Main street	Poor
Right	Warren street	Good
Left	Monument avenue	"
	MONUMENT	6 miles
Right	Chestnut street	Good
Cross	Chelsea street	Paved
Left	Wapping street	"

Navy Yard.

The monument is located in the Centre of Charlestown, and is reached by this route without passing over any paved or poor streets. The Navy Yard is open to visitors (week days) from 7.30 A. M. to 4.30 P. M. The Marine Museum contains many curiosities.

For a shorter route take right Dartmouth and Beacon streets, left Temple, cross Cambridge, through Staniford and Causeway to Warren avenue, over bridge to Common street then Winthrop to monument. Although much shorter than first route the streets are nearly all paved, and part of the way would have to be made on foot to avoid teams.

ROUTE THIRTY-SIX.

To Medfield, Medway, Millis and Milford.

	Copley square	
	Dartmouth street	Excellent
Right	Columbus avenue	Asphalt
Left	Camden street	Excellent
Right	Tremont street	Pavements
Left	Cabot street	Asphalt
Right	Hampshire street	Excellent
Left	Linden Park	"
Right	Elmwood street	"
Right	Roxbury street	"
Left	Pynchon street	"
	Centre street	"

JAMAICA PLAIN, 4 miles, left, South street, good, at Forest Hills take Washington street, excellent, ROS-LINDALE, 5 miles, right. South street good, left Centre street good, WEST ROXBURY, 7 miles, Spring street, good, Charles River, 8 miles, right, Bridge street, cross bridge. High street, good, WEST DEDHAM, 11 miles, right, Main street, good, MEDFIELD, 15 miles, Main street, Main street, Millis, 18 miles, Main street, W. MEDWAY, 22 miles Milford street, MILFORD, 27 miles.

ROUTE THIRTY-SEVEN.

To Milford.

Same as Route Twenty-three to South Framingham. SOUTH FRAMINGHAM, 18 miles, left, by Sherborn Prison, to East Holliston Depot, 22 miles, HOLLISTON (Washington street) 23 miles, BRAGGVILLE, 27 miles, MILFORD, 30 miles.

From South Framingham to Holliston the road is good; from there to Milford quite sandy or muddy, according to the weather.

G. N. HATCH & CO.,

CYCLE DEALERS

. . . AND . . .

ACCESSORIES.

WHEELS BUILT TO ORDER.

Machines Repaired, Enameled and Nickeled.

34 WARREN AVENUE, BOSTON.

F.W. BARRY. BEALE & CO.
STATIONERS,
108 & 110
Washington St.
Cor. ELM.
BOSTON.

ROUTE THIRTY-EIGHT.

To Reading.

	Copley square	
	Dartmouth street	Excellent
Left	Newbury street	
Right	W. Chester Park	"
Over	Harvard bridge	"
	Main street, CAMBRIDGE	"
Cross	Harvard square	3 miles
Left	North avenue	Good
	PORTER'S STATION	4 miles
Right	Russell street	Fair
Left	Elm street	"
Cross	R. R.	"
	Harvard street	"
Left	Medford street	"
	MEDFORD	7 1-2 miles
Cross	Mystic river	
Left	Fulton street	Good
	Wyoming avenue	Fair
	Pond street	"
Left	South street	"
	Main street	"
	STONEHAM	11 1-2 miles
	Main street	Fair
	READING	13 1-2 miles

Return, John street, fair, Lake Managowitt, Green street, fair, WAKEFIELD, 3 miles, Main street, fair, Crystal Lake, GREENWOOD, 3 3-4 miles, MELROSE, 5 miles, MALDEN, 7 3-4 miles. [See Malden for return to Boston.]

This route can be shortened by taking Forest street to Reading direct, but the road-bed this way is very poor.

ROUTE THIRTY-NINE.

Boston to Haverhill.

Route 59 to Beverly, 24 1-4 miles, Depot square, Rantoul street, good, follow horse car track, fair, NORTH BEVERLY, WENHAM, HAMILTON, IPSWICH, 35 3-4 miles, right, engine house, left, First street, good, ROWLEY, 40 miles, GEORGETOWN, side path, 46 1-2 miles, GROVELAND, side path, 50 miles, HAVERHILL, 53 1-4 miles.

Haverhill is a boot and shoe city of 25,000 population. The points of Interest are Public Library on Summer street, Whittier's birthplace, about three miles out on the Amesbury road, Lake Kenoza, and W. G. Wells' "Castle Winnekenni."

ROUTE FORTY.

Boston to New Bedford.

Same as route twelve to Brockton, WEST BRIDGE-WATER, 28 miles, BRIDGEWATER, 31 miles, NORTH MID-DLEBORO', 36 miles, LAKEVILLE, 40 miles, ACUSHNET, 53 miles, NEW BEDFORD, 57 miles.

From Middleboro' to Acushnet the roads are mostly unrideable and train is recommended if you ride a solid or cushion tire, but if you have a pneumatic, push through. The last five miles into New Bedford are good.

ROUTE FORTY-ONE.

To Mattapan.

Copley square, Dartmouth street, good, right, Columbus avenue, asphalt, left, W. Chester Park, excellent, right, Harrison avenue, good, left, Warren street, good, right, Walnut avenue, excellent, left, Dale street, excellent, right, Laurel street, excellent, left, Bower street, excellent, right, Warren street, good, left, Washington street, excellent, DORCHESTER, 6 1-2 miles, right, River street, excellent, MATTAPAN, 8 1-2 miles.

To return to Boston, continue on to Hyde Park, and then the reverse of Route 71.

ROUTE FORTY-TWO.

To Fitchburg.

Same as Route Twenty-Three to Northboro', NORTH-BORO', 34 miles, S. BERLIN, BERLIN, 38 1-2 miles, W. BERLIN, 40 miles, CLINTON, 42 1-2 miles, S. LANCASTER, No. LANCASTER, 46 3-4 miles, LEOMINSTER, 53 1-4 miles, FITCHBURG, 58 miles.

For Hudson [4 miles] turn to right at Berlin. The roads from Northboro' to Fitchburg are good, with few hills; through Lancaster they are exceptionally good.

ROUTE FORTY-THREE.

Boston to Walpole.

	Copley square	
	Huntington avenue	Excellent
Right	W. Chester Park	"
Left	Westland avenue	"
Left	Parker street	Good
Right	Centre street	"

JAMAICA PLAIN, 3 miles, right, by Soldiers' Monument, right, Weld street, excellent, left, Maple street, excellent, right, Centre street, good, WEST ROXBURY, 7 miles, through Dedham Centre, 10 miles, Washington street, good, NORWOOD, 16 miles, WALPOLE, 21 miles.

Moose Hill, 3 miles, commands a view of 60 towns. Massapoag Lake, 5 miles, Highland Lake Grove, 3 miles, Lake Pearl (Wrentham), 5 miles, are the points of interest.

ROUTE FORTY-FOUR.

Boston to Marblehead.

Same as Route Fifty-seven to Lynn Common.

	LYNN (Common)	16 3-4 miles
	North or South Common street	Good
Right	Market street	"
Left	Broad street	"

Follow Horse Railroad straight to Marblehead, 22 1-2 miles.

The run to Marblehead cannot be surpassed in this country, as the road is fine and the points of interest are many. Lee Mansion on Washington street, St. Michael's Church (built in 1714), Fort Sewall Park, Old Hill Burying Ground, off Beacon street, Old Brig, the birthplace of Moll Pitcher, and the Fountain Inn Well are all worth a visit. At Marblehead Neck, 1 1-2 miles, visit the Churn, Great Head, the lighthouse and Eastern Yacht Club House.

Brown's Bicycle Inn

178 COLUMBUS AVE.

The only boarding stable for Bicycles In Boston where you can leave or take your wheel at any hour of the day or evening.

Boston Agent for the AERIAL

Repairing and Renting   Bicycles Sold on Easy Terms

A Complete Assortment of Bicycle Sundries

COLUMBUS AVE. AGENT FOR

SINGER ✠ BICYCLES

NOTICE TO WHEELMEN

When visiting the Hub put your wheel up at the Inn, where you can have it cleaned and cared for.

ROUTE FORTY-FIVE.

To Providence R. I.

Copley square

	Huntington avenue	Excellent
Right	W. Chester Park	"
Left	Westland avenue	"
Left	Parker street	Good
Right	Centre street	"
	JAMAICA PLAIN	4 miles
Right	Weld street	Excellent
Left	Corey street	"
Right	Centre street	Good
Through	WEST ROXBURY	8 miles
Through	DEDHAM	10 miles

Washington street, good, NORWOOD, 16 miles, WAL-POLE, 21 miles, WRENTHAM 27 miles, PLAINVILLE, 32 miles, No. ATTLEBORO, 34 miles, DODGEVILLE, 40 miles, HEBRONVILLE, 44 miles, PAWTUCKET, 48 miles, PROVIDENCE, 53 miles.

There are almost as many routes to Providence as riders, but none better than this. The points of interest are Roger Williams Park, the Cove, Brown University, the Arcade, American Screw Company's Works, Quaker College, and many others.

ROUTE FORTY-SIX.

To Hough's Neck (Quincy.)

Same as Route Fifty-four to

	QUINCY	13 3-4 miles
Left	Coddington street	Good
Left	Sea street	"
	HOUGH'S NECK	17 miles

Hough's Neck is at the end of Quincy Peninsula, and is quite a summer resort, and is fast becoming a favorite rendezvous for bicyclers on account of its nearness to Boston and its fine fish dinners.

ROUTE FORTY-SEVEN.

To Newburyport.

Same as Route Fifty-nine to Beverly.

	Depot square	
	Rantoul street	Good
Follow	Horse-car Tracks to	
	WENHAM	
	HAMILTON	
	IPSWICH	13 miles
Right	Engine House	
Left	First street	Good
	ROWLEY	16 miles
Cross	Bridge	
	NEWBURY	23 miles
	Cemetery	
	High street	Good
	NEWBURYPORT	25 1-2 miles

This route was a part of the original 100 miles road race. The roads beyond Beverly are fully up to the average of country roads.

The points of interest are the homes of the French Refugees, the homesteads of the Wallaces, Caleb Cushing and Lord Timothy Dexter, the Old South Church, where Whitfield is buried, Public Library, where Washington was entertained, the home of Greely the Arctic explorer, residence of Gough, and Garden of the Dead.

ROUTE FORTY-EIGHT.

To Lawrence.

Same as Route Thirty-eight to Reading.

Main street	Good
ANDOVER	23 1-2 miles
LAWRENCE	30 miles

The roads beyond Reading are only fair. Wheelmen should visit the Pacific Mills (one of the largest in the world,) see the Lawrence Dam, and visit the reservoir, where a fine view of the city and surrounding country can be had.

To Portsmouth.

Same as Route Forty-seven to Newburyport, 49 3-4 miles, follow Horse-car track to Chain bridge, AMESBURY, 52 1-4 miles, SEABROOK, 53 1-4 miles, HAMPTON, 61 miles, PORTSMOUTH, 72 miles.

In wheeling towards Portsmouth, the Seabrook sands can be avoided by following the horse-car tracks from Newburyport, by the chain bridge, to Amesbury, instead of crossing the Merrimac River on the old travel bridge, near the railroad bridge at Newburyport. After crossing the Chain bridge wheelmen should take the second right turn at guide board marked " 18m. to Portsmouth," which road leads to the large Rocky Hill Meeting house, where a guide board is marked " Hampton, 9m.," which roads end at Methodist Church in Seabrook. Thence the regular travel road can be followed to Portsmouth. The trip from Boston to Portsmouth can be easily made in a day by any fair rider.

ROUTE FIFTY.

To Lowell and Nashua.

Same as Route Thirty-eight to Medford. MEDFORD, 8 3-4 miles, High street, Purchase street, WINCHESTER, 11 1-2 miles, follow Horse-car track to WOBURN, 14 1-2 miles, Winn street, BURLINGTON, 17 1-2 miles, Main road to BILLERICA, 23 miles, LOWELL, 30 miles, MIDDLESEX VILLAGE, 32 miles, TYNGSBORO, 36 1-2 miles, LITTLES, 39 1-2 miles, NASHUA, N. H., 42 1-2 miles.

The roads beyond Lowell are mostly poor.

ROUTE FIFTY-ONE.

To Fall River.

Same as Route Fifty-four to Brockton, 24 3-4 miles, Main street, good, right, W. Elm street, good, left, Warren avenue, right, Forrest avenue, good, right, by Fair grounds to Main street, good, No. EASTON, 28 3-4 miles, Hockamoch Swamp, NORTH RAYNHAM, 36 miles, TAUNTON, 39 miles, Somerset avenue to DIGHTON, 44 1-2 miles, SOMERSET, 50 miles, FALL RIVER, 55 miles.

From Taunton follow river on right bank all the way : roads not very good.

The
Oak Grove Farm Co.

Is in better position than ever to supply Family Trade in

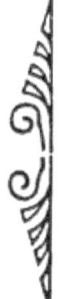

BOSTON

ROXBURY

DORCHESTER

LONGWOOD

BROOKLINE

CAMBRIDGE

With the Best of

Dairy Products

and also

Unexcelled Ice Cream

BOSTON

80 Ruggles Street   445 Boylston Street

CAMBRIDGE

496 Main Street   434 Harvard Street

Ask us to supply you with Artificial Ice

ROUTE FIFTY-TWO.

Chestnut Hill Reservoir to Dedham.

	Reservoir	
Right	Beacon street	Good
Left	Hammond street	Excellent
Left	Newton street	"
Right	South street	"
	Church street	Good
Right	Centre street	
	WEST ROXBURY	7 miles
Right	Spring street	Good
	Charles River	
	Bridge street	
Left	Ames street	Good
	Charles River	
	Washington street	Good
	DEDHAM	10 miles

ROUTE FIFTY-THREE.

Copley Sq. to Auburndale, via Reservoir Road.

	Copley square	
	Dartmouth street	
Left	Commonwealth avenue	Excellent
Right	Gloucester street	"
Left	Beacon street	"
Right	Chestnut avenue	
Left	South street	"
Right	Ward street	"
Left	Centre street	"
Right	Homer street	"
	Fuller street	Fair
Right	Woodlawn street	
	AUBURNDALE	9 miles

Return to Washington street, and via Newton to Boston.

ROUTE FIFTY-FOUR.

To Brockton.

	Copley square	
	Dartmouth street	Good
Right	Columbus avenue	Asphalt
Left	Chester Park	Excellent
Right	Boston street	Good
Left	Hancock street	
Left	Adams street	Excellent
	DORCHESTER	
Cross	Neponset River Bridge	

MILTON LOWER MILLS, 6 3-4 miles, Milton Hill, Adams street, excellent, EAST MILTON, 8 1-2 miles, QUINCY, 11 miles, BRAINTREE, 13 miles, SOUTH BRAINTREE, 14 miles, RANDOLPH, 18 3-4 miles, EAST STOUGHTON, 21 miles, BROCKTON, 24 3-4 miles.

For Stoughton [3 miles] take Pond street (right) at E. Stoughton, then right, Central street, left, Lincoln street, to Stoughton centre.

ROUTE FIFTY-FIVE.

To Cobb's Tavern.

Copley square, Dartmouth street, good, right, Columbus avenue, asphalt, left, W. Chester Park, excellent, Swett street, good, right, Boston street, good, Columbia street, good, left, Washington street, Codman Hill, DORCHESTER, 6 1-4 miles, cross Neponset River bridge, MILTON LOWER MILLS, 6 1-2 miles, Milton Hill, right, Central avenue, good, Washington street, good, PONKAPOAG, right, Washington street, good, CANTON, Cobb's Tavern, 16 1-2 miles.

At the top of Milton Hill an excellent view of Boston Harbor and Massachusetts Bay and of the surrounding country is afforded. Codman Hill has a short, stiff grade which should be coasted carefully. Cobb's Tavern has the appearance of a farm house of a century ago, and is well known to Boston cyclists for its fine dinners.

ROUTE FIFTY-SIX.

Boston to Milton and Quincy.

Copley square, Dartmouth street, good, right, Columbus avenue, asphalt, left, W. Chester Park, excellent, left, Swett street, good, right, Boston street, good, Columbia street, good, left, Washington street, excellent, Codman Hill, DORCHESTER, 6 1-2 miles, Neponset River bridge, MILTON LOWER MILLS, 6 1-2 miles, Milton Hill, Adams street, excellent, EAST MILTON, 8 1-2 miles, Blue Hill, QUINCY, 11 1-2 miles.

Milton Hill is a very hard climb, and should only be coasted by skillful riders, and with brake on. Quincy is the home of the Adams family, and in the neighborhood are many points of historical interest, especially connected with the " Family of Presidents."

ROUTE FIFTY-SEVEN

To Nahant.

Copley square

	Dartmouth street,	Excellent
Left	Newbury street	"
Right	W. Chester Park	"
Over	Harvard Bridge	
	Main street, CAMBRIDGE	

Cross Harvard square, 3 miles, left, North avenue, good, PORTER'S STATION, 4 miles, right, Russell street, fair, left, Elm street, fair, cross Broadway, fair, Harvard street, fair, left, Medford street, fair, MEDFORD, 7 1-2 miles, right, Salem street, good, MALDEN, 9 1-2 miles, MAPLEWOOD, 11 miles, EAST SAUGUS, 14 3-4 miles, LYNN (Common,) 16 3-4 miles, North or South Common street, good, right, Market street, good, left, Broad street, good, right, Newhall street, good, right, Lower Beach Road, good, Hood Cottage, Bass Point House, Relay House, NAHANT, 19 3-4 miles.

At Malden Pump, take Ferry street, left, Elm street, for Woodlawn Cemetery.

This route can be considerably shortened by taking Chelsea Ferry (foot of Hanover street,) to Chelsea, and as follows :

BERLO RACER

PETER J. BERLO⊙

BUILDER OF LIGHT WEIGHT

High . Grade . Cycles

Racers 15 to 20 lbs.
Roadsters 22 to 28 lbs.

Difficult Repair Work Promptly Executed

AGENCY FOR

The P. K. Tire Co.

MANUFACTURER OF

LIGHT WEIGHT TIRES

Racing Tires a Specialty

PNEUMATIC TIRES REPAIRED

48 Columbus Ave. Boston

Chelsea Ferry, CHELSEA, Winnisimmet street, poor, left, Beacon street, fair, right, Chestnut street, (coast) good, left, Fifth street, good, right, Spruce street, good, right, Washington avenue, fair, Cary avenue, good, left, Clark avenue, good, right. Eleanor street, good, left, Broadway, good, REVERE. LYNN (Common.)

Nahant is a beautiful and aristocratic watering place, with superb ocean views and breezes. The ocean roads are very good. Points of interest are Pirates' Cave, Maolis Gardens, Natural Bridge, Pulpit Rock, Spouting Horn and Cauldron Cliff. The return may be made by steamer, giving a good chance to see the harbor.

ROUTE FIFTY-EIGHT.

To South Natick.

Copley square.

	Dartmouth street	Excellent
Left	Commonwealth avenue	"
Left	Beacon street	"
Pass	Chestnut hill reservoir	5 miles
	Beacon street	Excellent
	Great Sign Boards	10 miles
	NEWTON LOWER FALLS	10 3-4 miles
	WELLESLEY HILLS	12 1-2 miles
	WELLESLEY	13 1-4 miles
	Washington street	Good
	SOUTH NATICK	16 miles

This vicinity is rich in historical points of interest. In the square where now stands the drinking fountain once stood the oak under which John Eliot, the Indian apostle, weekly gathered together the first Indian Church, after the flight from Nonantum Hill. A large tree near by goes by the name of "Eliot's Oak," in commemoration of these meetings, and directly opposite the hotel, in the green, stands Eliot Memorial Monument. The roads into the city are of the very highest sand-papered variety.

To Gloucester.

Copley square

	Dartmouth street	Excellent
	Newbury street	"
Left	W. Chester Park	"
Right	Harvard bridge	"
Over	Main street, CAMBRIDGE	"

Cross Harvard square. 3 miles, left North avenue, good, PORTER'S STATION, 4 miles, right, Russell street, fair, left, Elm street, fair, cross, Broadway, fair, Harvard street, fair, left, Medford street, good, MEDFORD, 7 1-2 miles, right, Salem street, good, MALDEN, 9 1-2 miles, MAPLEWOOD, 11 miles, EAST SAUGUS, 13 3-4 miles, LYNN (Common), 16 3-4 miles, Common street, fair, Essex street, fair, Lafayette street, good, right, Essex street, good, Essex House, Salem, 22 3-4 miles, St. Peter's street, good, right, Brown street, good, left, Winter street, good, Bridge street, good, Bridge, Rantoul street, good, BEVERLY, 24 1-4 miles, Bow street, good, Soldiers' Monument, left, Hale street, good, Pride's crossing, 26 1-2 miles, BEVERLY FARMS, 27 miles, MANCHESTER BY THE SEA, 29 3-4 miles, MAGNOLIA, 32 1-2 miles, GLOUCESTER, 47 miles.

Gloucester is the most important of Massachusetts fishing ports, and sends out about 650 vessels. The harbor is very large and deep, and quite picturesque in appearance. The principal points of interest are the stone quarries at Bay View and Lanesville, at the northern part of the cape, the Eastern Point Lighthouse and Old Fort at East Gloucester, Bass Rocks, Good Harbor Beach and the summer houses at East Gloucester. A pleasant bicycle ride of fifteen miles is "Around the Cape," taking in Rockport, Pigeon Cove, Bay View, Lanesville, Annisquam, Riverdale and thence to Gloucester. The Willow roads at Lanesville and Riverdale are both worth a trip to see. Phillips avenue at Pigeon Cove, on the most extreme end of Cape Ann, affords a charming view of the ocean. The Pavilion Hotel, Western avenue, facing Main street, is the best in the city, and caters especially to visiting wheelmen at reasonable rates.

ROUTE SIXTY.

Chestnut Hill Reservoir, to Dedham.

	Reservoir	
	Beacon street	Good
Left	Hammond street,	Excellent
Left	Newton street	"
Right	South street	"
	Church street	Good
Right	Centre street	"
	WEST ROXBURY	5 1-4 miles
Right	Spring street	Good
	Charles River	.
	Bridge street	
Left	Ames street	Good
	Charles River	
	Washington street	Good
	Dedham	7 3-4 miles

ROUTE SIXTY-ONE.

To Walpole.

	Copley square	
	Huntington avenue	Excellent
Right	W. Chester Park	"
Left	Westland avenue	"
Left	Parker street	Good
Right	Centre street	"
	JAMAICA PLAIN	3 miles

Right, by Soldier's Monument, right, Weld street, excellent, left, Maple street, excellent, right, Centre street, good, WEST ROXBURY, 7 miles, through Dedham Centre, 10 miles, Washington street, good, NORWOOD, 14 miles, WALPOLE, 19 miles.

ROUTE SIXTY-TWO.

To Albany, N. Y.

Route Forty-two to

Fitchburg, 58 miles, River street under R. R. West Fitchburg, road fair, 59 1-2 miles, Westminster, good, 66 miles, South Gardener, fair, 68 3-4 miles, East Templeton, poor, 72 1-4 miles, Templeton, fair, 74 miles, Brooks Village, fair, 75 3-4 miles, Athol, fair, 82 miles, Orange, poor, 89 miles, West Orange, poor, 91 miles, Erving, poor, 93 miles, Farley, poor, 96 miles, Millers Falls, poor, 99 1-2 miles, Turner's Falls, fair, 104 1-2 miles, Greenfield, fair, 108 1-2 miles, Shelburn, poor, 113 1-2 miles, Shelburn Falls, poor, 117 miles, East Charlemont poor, 121 miles, follow Greenfield River all the way to Hoosac Tunnel, 135 miles, through Charlemont, 126 miles, Zoar, 131 miles, North Adams, hilly, 145 miles, Williamstown, fair, 152 miles, North Pownal Vt., fair, 159 miles, N. Petersburg N. Y. fair, 164 miles, Troy, N. Y. fair, 188 miles, Albany N. Y., fair, 195 miles.

ROUTE SIXTY-THREE.

To Keene, N. H.

Route Forty-two to

Fitchburg, fair, 58 miles, West Fitchburg, good, 59 1-2 miles, Westminster, good, 65 miles, South Gardener, good, 86 miles, Gardener, poor, 70 miles, Winchenden, poor, 80 miles, Fitzwilliam, N. H. poor, 89 miles, Troy, N. H. poor 94 miles, Marlboro N. H. poor, 100 miles, Keene, N. H. poor, 106 miles.

ROUTE SIXTY-FOUR.

Gloucester to Gloucester, around Cape Ann.

Left	Pavilion Hotel	
	Washington street	Good
	RIVERDALE	2 miles
	Holly street	
	ANNISQUAM	3 3-4 miles

Right	Bennett street	
	BAY VIEW	5 miles
	LANESVILLE	7 miles
	PIGEON COVE	8 1-4 miles
	Granite street	Good
	ROCKPORT	10 miles
	Main street	Good
	Eastern avenue	"
	Main street	"
	PAVILION HOTEL	14 3-4 miles

This route is what is known as around the cape and although hilly is of unusual interest and is in sight of the ocean all the way.

ROUTE SIXTY-FIVE.

To Hartford, Conn.
Same as Route Twenty-three to

WORCESTER, 45 miles, same as route sixty-nine to SPRINGFIELD, Main street, good, 106 miles, THOMPSONVILLE, good, 113 1-2 miles, ENFIELD, good, 115 1-2 miles, WAREHOUSE POINT, good, 117 1-2 miles, EAST HARTFORD, good, 130 miles, HARTFORD, good, 132 miles.

ROUTE SIXTY-SIX.

To South Natick, via Echo Bridge, via Route Twenty-one to Echo Bridge.

Left	Chestnut street	Good
Left	Boylston street, old B. & W. Turnpike	"
	WELLESLEY HILLS	13 miles
	WELLESLEY	14 1-2 miles
Left	Washington street	Good
	SOUTH NATICK	16 3-4 miles

ROUTE SIXTY-SEVEN.

To Boston via. Watertown, Arlington and Medford.

	Copley square	
	Boylston street	Excellent
Right	W. Chester Park	..
Left	through Back Bay Park	"
	Commonwealth avenue	"
	ALLSTON	3 miles
	N. Beacon street	
	BRIGHTON	4 1-4 miles
Right	Market street,	Excellent
Left	Arsenal street	"
Right	Coolidge avenue	"
	HILL'S CROSSING	7 1-2 miles
Left	Grove street	Excellent
Right	Brighton street	"
Right	Pleasant street	"
	ARLINGTON	9 1-4 miles
	Height street to	Excellent
	MEDFORD	12 miles

Return to Boston by reverse of route 30. This route is a very interesting one and the roads are superb.

ROUTE SIXTY-EIGHT.

To Boston via. Milton, Hyde Park, E. Dedham, Dedham, Dedham and Needham.

	Same as ROUTE TWELVE to	
	MILTON LOWER MILLS	6 1-2 miles
Right	River street	Excellent
	MATTAPAN	7 3-4 miles
	HYDE PARK	9 3-4 miles
	River street	Excellent
	EAST DEDHAM	11 3-4 miles
Left	High street	Excellent
	DEDHAM	12 3-4 miles
	High street	Excellent
Right	Common street	"
	West street	"
	Dedham street	"
	NEEDHAM	16 3-4 miles
Right	Highland avenue	Excellent
	to Newton Centre	
Right	Beacon street to Boston	27 miles

This route is over some of the finest roads in Eastern Mass.

ROUTE SIXTY-NINE.

To Springfield.
Same as Route Twenty-three to

Worcester, Main street, road good, 45 miles, New Worcester, road good, 47 miles, Valley Falls, road good, 48 miles, Cherry Valley, road good, 49 1-2 miles, Leicester, road poor, 51 1-2 miles, Spencer, road poor, 57 miles, East Brookfield, road fair, 60 miles, Brookfield, road fair, 64 miles, West Brookfield, road fair, 66 1-2 miles, Warren, road fair, 70 miles, Palmer, road fair, 81 miles, North Wilbraham, road fair, 95 miles, Indian Orchard, road fair, 99 1-2 miles, Springfield, road fair, 106 miles.

To Boston via Worcester and Providence, R. I.
Same as Route Twenty-three to

Worcester, Milbury street, road good, 45 miles, Milbury, road good, 51 miles, Wilkinsonville, road good, 53 miles, Fishville, road good, 54 miles, Farnumsville, road good, 55 1-2 miles, Rockdale, road good, 57 miles, Whitings Station, road good, 62 1-2 miles, Uxbridge, road good, 63 1-2 miles, Millville, road poor, 69 miles. Blackstone, road poor, 71 1-2 miles, Woonsocket, R. I., road good, 74 miles, Cumberland Hill, road poor, 77 miles, Ashton, road excellent, 80 miles, Berkeley, road excellent, 81 miles, Lonsdale, road excellent, 83 miles, Valley Falls, road excellent, 85 miles, Pawtucket, road excellent, 87 miles, Providence, R. I., road excellent, 92 miles.

Return to Boston by reverse of route forty-five, total distance 145 miles.

ROUTE SEVENTY.

To Revere and Crescent Beaches, Beachmont, Ocean Spray, Great Head and Point Shirley.

	Copley square	
	Dartmouth street	Excellent
Left	Newbury street	..
Right	W. Chester Park	..
Over	Harvard Bridge	..
	Main street, CAMBRIDGE	
Cross	Harvard square	3 miles

Left	North avenue	Good
	PORTER'S STATION	4 miles
Right	Russell street	Fair
Left	Elm street	..
Cross	Broadway	..
	Harvard street	..
Left	Medford street	Good
	MEDFORD	7 1-2 miles
Right	Salem street	Good
	MALDEN	9 1-2 miles
	MAPLEWOOD	11 miles
	Linden square	Good
Right	Washington avenue	..
Left	Malden street	
Left	Beach street	..
	Depot	13 3-4 miles
Right	Beach Road	
To	⎧ BEACHMONT ⎪ OCEAN SPRAY ⎨ GREAT HEAD ⎪ POINT SHIRLEY	
Left	Beach Board at Depot for	
	Crescent Beach	
	Point of Pines	15 3-4 miles

Or take **East Boston**, North Ferry, EAST BOSTON,
Maverick square, **Meridian** street, **good**, right, Saratoga
street, good, **right**, WINTHROP JUNCTION, Main **street**,
WINTHROP, OCEAN SPRAY.

———

To return from Ocean Spray, cross the bridge at
Great Head run through Winthrop village, to the bridge
and to **the Winthrop Junction.**

All of these places lie along the North Shore, and
are about a mile apart. The roads in the vicinity of the
beaches **are in good condition and** attract many wheelmen hither during the warm months.

Boston can be reached from all these resorts by fre-
quent trains of the Boston Revere Beach and Lynn Railroad, which carries *Bicycles free.*

A BICYCLE OF

THE

HIGHEST

GRADE

Puritan

TRADE MARK

Manufactured by

O. J. FAXON & CO.

3 Appleton Street

BOSTON, MASS.

To Arnold Arboretum and Hyde Park.

Copley square

	Dartmouth street	Good
Right	Columbus avenue	Asphalt
Left	W. Chester Park	Excellent
Right	Harrison avenue	Good
Left	Warren street	"
Right	Walnut avenue	Excellent
Through	Franklin Park	
Right	Morton street	Good
	Forest Hills Station	3 1-2 miles
Cross	Old Colony R. R.	
	Arnold Aboretum	
	Bussey Farm	
Left	South street	
Right	Washington street	
	Roslindale	4 1-2 miles
Left	Poplar street	Good
Left	Canterbury street	"
Right	Hyde Park Avenue	"
	Clarendon Hills	5 1-2 miles
	Hyde Park	6 1-2 miles

Return from Arnold Arboretum. Centre street to Pond street. Then Route 34; from Hyde Park one good way is by River street to Mattapan, and reverse of route 41.

At the Arboretum and Farm is a nearly exhaustive collection of shrubs and herbaceous plants possible to be grown in the open air in this climate. The Bussey Farm is the agricultural and horticultural department of Harvard University.

Only members showing ticket can procure privileges.
The rates are on the card of appointment and will be
shown on application.

Ashland — Central House.
Attleboro — Park Hotel.
Andover — The Elm.
Arlington — Arlington House.
Abington — Keene's.

Auburndale, Mass. WOODLAND PARK HOTEL
JOSEPH LEE, Propr.
Rate per Day $3.00.   Rate per Week $15.00

Bedford — Bedford House.
Brookfield — The Brookfield House.
Boston — The Grand Hotel, 417 Columbus avenue.
Brockton — Hotel Belmont.
Clinton — The Clinton House.
Concord — Thoreau House.
Danvers — The Hotel Danvers.
Dedham — Norfolk House.
Fall River — The Mellen House.
East Boston — Maverick House.
East Bridgewater — American House.
Fitchburg — The American House.
Florence — Hotel Florence.
Franklin — Hotel Darling.
Framingham — Wheeler House.
Gardner — Gardner House.   Richards' Hotel.
Georgetown — Pentucket House.
Greenfield — Mansion House.
Great Barrington — Miller House.
Haverhill — Bartlett House.
Holbrook — Adams' Boarding House.
Holliston — Hotel Bullard.
Holyoke — The Hamilton.
Hopkinton — Park House.
Ipswich — The Agawam.
Jamaica Plain—Restaurant, Green and Oakdale streets.
Lynn — Revere House.
Lowell — American House.
Leicester — Leicester Hotel.
Leominster — Leominster Hotel.
Ludlow — Hunt's Boarding House.
Medford — Medford House.

Milford — The William.
Maynard — The Maple House.
Malden — Evelyn House.
Millbury — The Tourtelotte.
Manchester — Manchester House.
Monson — The Monson House.

Marlboro, Mass.   WINDSOR HOUSE,
L. HOUDE, Propr.
Rate per Day $2.00.   Special Rate by the Week.

New Bedford — The Mansion House.
Newton — Woodland Park Hotel.

Newburyport, Mass.   WOLFE' TAVERN,
FOWLE & JOHNSTON, Proprietors
Per Day $2.50 & $3.00   Per Week $14.00 to $21.00

North Easton — Packard House.
North Adams — Richmond House.
Norwood — Norwood House.
Norton — Mansion House.
Palmer — Weeks House.
Pittsfield — American House.
Plymouth — Central House.
Quincy — Robertson House.
Rockland — Hotel Jackson.
Rockport — Rockport House.
Salem — Essex House.
South Framingham — Winthrop House.
Shelburne — Shelburne Falls House.
South Egremont — Mt. Everett.
Spencer — Massasoit.
Springfield — Haynes Hotel. Barrs Restaurant.
Taunton — City Hotel.
Templeton — Templeton House.
Upton — Mt. Peasant House.
Waltham — Prospect House.
Wareham — Kendrick House.
Warren — Warren Hotel.
Webster — Joslin House.
Westboro — Whitney House.
Westfield — Central House.
Westport — Hotel Westport.
Whittinsville — Whittinsville Hotel.
Winchendon — American House.
Woburn — Central House.
Worcester — Commonwealth Hotel.
Woods Holl — Dexter House.

The Proper Dress for a Lady.

A bicycle dress should be made either of flannel or ladies' cloth; the color should be dark—black or dark blue preferred. In making your dress, have it the ordinary walking length, or about two inches from the floor. The skirt should not be over two and a half yards wide, and should be faced eighteen to twenty inches from the bottom (all the way 'round) with same material or something equally heavy, to make it hang nicely, and to prevent the pedal from catching in the hem. Use no dress braid around the bottom of the skirt.

Do not wear flowing or loose sleeves—have them moderately tight.

Do not wear corsets, as you cannot jump or climb hills with any comfort in them. Wear a tight-fitting healthwaste instead. Mrs. Foy's health-waist is the best. It is not advisable to wear a bustle.

Wear heavy woolen underwear in cold weather and not many skirts.

Wear a turban; or, better yet, a close-fitting, light cap, similar to those worn by wheelmen. Don't wear a large and heavy hat or anything that will catch the wind.

"All under-clothing should be made of wool; linen and muslin are as uncomfortable as they are dangerous. I can heartily recommend the gray woolen combination made in Scotland, which is neither clumsy nor complicated. Corsets made of wool are now to be had, and very sensible corsets they are with but few bones and little stiffness."—*A writer in Harper's Bazar.*

"Let me, however, say, by way of preface, that the dress best adapted to cycling is the most suitable for all out-of-door amusement and healthy exercise. Therefore I am not addressing myself to cyclers only, but to every sensible woman who believes in rational dress; that is, using the term in its real sense, and not merely in its narrowest acceptation, when it means a divided skirt or other like abominations."—*A writer in Harper's Bazar.*

"It is generally an accepted fact that a neat, quiet, walking dress, with kilted skirt and well-cut body, either of the coat or Norfolk jacket type, is the best for riding. If the gown is neat,—very neat and correct as a walking gown,—it is quite right for the machine, as the rest is a matter of personal carriage and attention."—*London Queen*.

Both in winter and summer all clothing of cyclers should be of wool. A Norfolk jacket and pleated skirt of gray cloth and a soft Alpine hat are very becoming to a lady. Norfolk jacket and knickerbockers, or lounge jacket and knee breeches or trousers, for gentlemen. Wear shoes, not boots, which interfere with the free play of the ankles.

There are dozens of times in every winter when wheeling is even better than during the warm season. Don't be in a hurry to put your wheel away; keep it ready for just such an emergency; try the smooth, frost-bound roads. Thick clothing and gloves, together with a brisk pace, will soon send the blood rushing through your veins in healthy flow. . . . . . Some of the very finest riding I have ever seen was over the frost-hardened roads around the suburbs of Boston. Where the frost had been hard, the ground bare, and the traffic had smoothed down the "hubbles," the surface becomes as smooth as a race track. Keep your wheel out this winter and take a whirl when the surfaces permit. It will pay you."

1893 - - BICYCLE RECORDS - - 1893

AMERICAN RECORDS

AGAINST TIME.

DISTANCE.	NAME.	PLACE.	TIME.
1-4 Mile, standing....	Geo. F. Taylor,	Hartford, July 5, '92,	.32 1-5*
1-2 " "	W. W. Windle,	Springfield, Oct. 8, '92	1.03 3-5*
3-4 " "	W. W. Windle,	Springfield, Oct. 8, '92	1.34 *
1 " "	W. W. Windle,	Springfield, Oct. 8, '92,	2.05 3-5*
2 " "	W. W. Windle,	Springfield, Sept. 30, '92,	4.28 3-5*
3 " "	W. W. Windle,	Springfield, Sept. 29, '92,	7.04 3-5*
4 " "	W. W. Windle,	Springfield, Sept. 29, '92,	9.26 3-5*
5 " "	W. W. Windle,	Springfield, Sept. 29, '92,	11.41 ▶ *
6 " "	Hoyland Smith,	Hartford, July, 5, '92,	15.11 1-5
7 " "	Hoyland Smith.	Hartford, July, 5, '92,	17.49 3-5
8 " "	Hoyland Smith,	Hartford, July, 5, '92,	20.27
9 " "	Hoyland Smith,	Hartford, July, 5, '92,	23.04 4-5
10 " "	Hoyland Smith,	Hartford, July, 5, '92,	25.35 2-5
375 Miles less 150 yards	F. E. Spooner	Chicago, July 9, '92,	24 hours

FLYING START, AGAINST TIME.

1-4 mile.............	H. C. Tyler	Springfield, July 14, '92,	.28 2-5
1-2 "	W. W. Windle,	Springfield, Oct. 8, '92,	.57 4-5
3-4 "	W. W. Windle,	Springfield, Oct. 7, '92,	1.30 4-5
1 "	W. W. Windle,	Springfield, Oct. 7, '92,	2.02 3-5

IN COMPETITION

1-4 Mile, flying start	A. A. Zimmerman,	Hartford, Sept. 6, '92,	.27 *
1-4 " standing "	G. C. Smith,	Hartford, Sept. 6, '92,	.31 1-5*
1-2 " " "	A. A. Zimmerman,	Hartford, Sept. 6, '92,	1.01 4-5*
3-4 " " "	Geo. F. Taylor	Springfield, Sept. 15, '92,	1.41 1-5*
1 " " "	Geo. F. Taylor,	Springfield, Sept. 15, '92,	2.15 2-5*
2 " " "	A. A. Zimmerman,	Springfield, Sept. 13, '92,	4.51 *
3 " " "	L. D. Munger,	Evansville, Ind.Oct.6,'92,	7.38 3-5*
4 " " "	L. D. Munger,	Evansville, Ind.Oct.6,'92,	10.13 1-5*
5 " " "	A. E. Lumsden,	Evansville, Ind.Oct.6,'92,	12.36 3-5*
6 " " "	C. Ford Seeley,	New York, July 9, '92,	18.40 2-5
7 " " "	Carl Hess,	New York, July 9, '92,	21.45 2-5
8 " " "	Hoyland Smith,	New York, July 9, '92,	24.45 3-5
9 " " "	R. W. Steves,	New York, July 9, '92,	28.03 3-5
10 " " "	P. J. Berlo,	New York, July 9, '92,	30.40 2-5

*World's Records.

KITE TRACK RECORDS

1-4 Mile, flying start	J. S. Johnson,	Independence, Sept.16,'92	.26 1-5
1-4 " standing "	J. S. Johnson,	Independence, Sept.17,'92	.30
1-2 " flying "	J. S. Johnson,	Independence, Sept.17,'92	.55 1-2
1-2 " standing "	J. S. Johnson,	Independence, Sept.20,'92	.58 3-5
1 " flying "	J. S. Johnson,	Independence, Sept.22,'92	1.56 3-5
1 " standing "	J. S. Johnson,	Independence, Sept.20,'92	2.04 3-5

ENGLISH RECORDS.

DISTANCE.	NAME.	PLACE.	TIME.
1-4 Mile, flying start	J. W. Schofield,	Putney,	.29 2-5
1-4 " standing "	J. W. Schofield,	Putney,	.31 1-5
1-2 " " "	J. W. Schofield,	Putney,	1.02
3-4 " " "	J. W. Schofield,	Putney,	1.38 2-5
1 " " "	A. W. Harris,	Herne Hill,	2.12 3-5
2 " " "	M. B. Fowler,	Herne Hill,	4.49 4-5
3 " " "	M. B. Fowler,	Herne Hill,	7.16 2-5
4 " " "	M. B. Fowler,	Herne Hill,	9.47 1-5
5 " " "	M. B. Fowler,	Herne Hill,	12.16 1-5
10 " " "	F. J. Osmond,	Herne Hill,	24.50 1-5
413 3-4 Miles.........	F. W. Shorland,	Herne Hill Track,	24 hours

World's Record for 24 hours on the track was made September 14, 1892, 418 miles 1320 yards, by Stephane at Paris.

World's Record on the Road, 366 1-2 miles for 24 hours, by F. W. Shorland.

HOW EASY IT IS TO FORGET

I was born........................... 189

At ....

My weight was......... ....pounds, on...... 189

Height.. ....

The number on the case of my watch is.........................

The number on the works is........... ....

The number of my bank book is ....

Size of Hat ....Shoes.............Gloves...............

   "   Collar..............Cuffs.......... ....Hose ....

   "   Shirt ....Undershirt ....Drawers ....

IDENTIFICATION.

My name is ....

Address...

....

In case of serious accident to me, please notify...................

....

....

The number of my bicycle is.......... ....

Maker.................................... ....

Bought of..

My L. A. W. number is...

Record of Miles Ridden during 189

DAYS	JAN.	FEB.	MARCH	APRIL	MAY	JUNE
1						
2						
3						
4						
5						
6						
7						
8						
9						
10						
11						
12						
13						
14						
15						
16						
17						
18						
19						
20						
21						
22						
23						
24						
25						
26						
27						
28						
29						
30						
31						

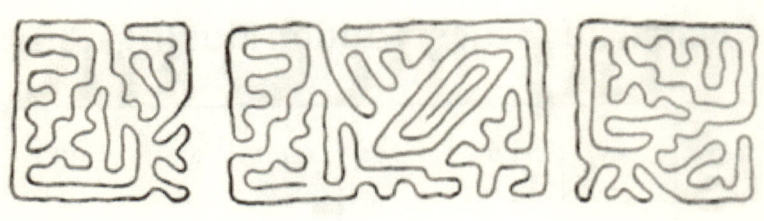

Have you ever ridden a

McCune Wheel?

If not, try one at once, and notice how quick it responds to the least application of power.

See Cut on back of this page.

The McCune Cycle Co.

47 Franklin St., = = Boston.

The McCune

LARGE TUBING   LARGE BALLS, 7-16

Weight Stripped, 26 1-2 lbs.

Weight, all on, 28 lbs.

Price, Stripped, $140.   With Brake and Coasters, $150.

The McCune Cycle Co.

47 FRANKLIN STREET - - - BOSTON

Record of Miles Ridden during 189

JULY	AUG.	SEPT.	OCT.	NOV.	DEC.	DAYS
						1
						2
						3
						4
						5
						6
						7
						8
						9
						10
						11
						12
						13
						14
						15
						16
						17
						18
						19
						20
						21
						22
						23
						24
						25
						26
						27
						28
						29
						30
						31

HELP! In Case of Accidents.

Drowning. **1.** Loosen clothing, if any, **2.** Empty lungs of water by laying body on its stomach and lifting it by the middle so that the head hangs down. Jerk the body a few times. **3.** Pull tongue forward, using handkerchief, or pin with string, if necessary **4.** Imitate motion of respiration by alternately compressing and expanding the lower ribs, about twenty times a minute. Alternately raising and lowering the arms from the sides up above the head will stimulate the action of the lungs. Let it be done gently but persistently. **5.** Apply warmth and friction to extremities. **6.** By holding tongue forward, closing the nostrils and pressing the "Adams apple" back, (so as to close entrance to stomach), direct inflation may be tried. Take a deep breath and breath it forcibly into mouth of patient, compress the chest to expel the air, and repeat the operation. **7.** DON'T GIVE UP! People have been saved after hours of patient, vigorous effort. **8.** When breathing begins, get patient into a warm bed, give warm drinks, or spirits in teaspoonfuls. Fresh air and quiet.

Lightning. Dash cold water over a person struck.

Sunstroke. Loosen clothing. Get patient into shade and apply ice-cold water to head.

Mad Dog or Snake Bite. Tie cord tight above wound. Suck the wound and cauterize with caustic or white-hot iron at once, or cut out adjoining parts with a sharp knife.

Venomous Insects' Stings, etc. Apply weak Ammonia. Oil, Salt Water, or Iodine.

Fainting. Place flat on back; allow fresh air and sprinkle with water.

Tests of Death. Hold mirror to mouth. If living, moisture will gather. Push pin into flesh. If dead the hole will remain, if alive it will close up.

Cinders in the Eye. Roll soft paper up like a lamp lighter and wet the tip to remove, or use a medicine dropper to draw it out. Rub the *other eye*.

Fire in one's Clothing. *Don't run*,—especially not down stairs or out of doors. Roll on carpet, or wrap in woolen rug or blanket. Keep the head down, so as not to inhale flame.

Fire in a Building. Crawl on the floor. The clearest air is the lowest in the room. Cover head with a woolen wrap, if possible. Cut holes for the eyes. Don't get excited.

Fire in Kerosene. *Don't use water*, it will spread the flames. Dirt, sand or flour are the best extinguishers; or smother with woolen rug, table-cloth or carpet.

Wounded or severed Veins. A vein is known to be wounded when dark blood flows in a rapid and uniform stream from the seat of injury. Apply cold compress and fasten tightly with roller bandage.

When an artery is cut or wounded, the blood is of a rich scarlet or ruby red color and comes in regular spurts. *Immediately* and *tightly* compress the surface of the nearest convenient spot between the wound and the heart, and apply ice or cold water, use styptics, such as pulverized alum, gallic acid, etc,, and send for a physician at once. Time is life in such a case.

As impromptu, but efficient compress, is made by tying the ends of a handkerchief together, placing it at the desired point of compression, and twisting as tightly as possible by means of a stick used as a lever.

THE CARE OF A MACHINE.

A good bicycle, like a good horse, deserves the best of care; for although the expense of keeping a first class machine in repair, so far as breakage is concerned, is very slight, still it deteriorates rapidly in selling value if not kept clean and in good order. You may want to exchange or sell your wheel sometime, when you will find that the condition of its finish regulates the price you can get for it more than any other point. Therefore, make a point of keeping the nickel bright; use Putz' pomade or nickel polishing paste, such as will be found at every cycling agency. Wash the mud or dust off the enamel with a sponge or soft rag, and wipe it dry with a piece of Canton flannel; use Canton flannel also in applying the polishing paste. By making a point of cleaning your wheel at least once a week, it will be but a few moments work and your machine will always look bright and nice; but if you put it off the nickel will rust, and you will find it no easy task to restore it to its original lustre.

"Apparel oft proclaims the man:" so, too, a rider is frequently judged by his wheel and the condition in which he keeps it. It pays in dollars and cents, you will find, to keep your wheel bright and clean, besides the satisfaction of riding a machine that looks as if it had not been bought in a junk shop.

Use only the best oil on the bearings. This is important. A poor oil will gum the bearings and make the machine run hard. It is better to buy oil at a cycle agency for the reason that you will be sure of getting oil that has been thoroughly tested and known to be adapted to the purpose. It costs no more than the common sewing machine or drug store oil, and under the new postal regulations, may be sent by mail, hence you will be wise to buy your bicycle oil at a bicycle house only.

The ball bearings of a first class machine are as finely made as a watch. Every part is gauged to the 2000th part of an inch, and is put together with the greatest exactitude. These bearings should be kept clean and well oiled. By this we do not mean that they should be kept dripping with oil or that they should be oiled very often. A good plan will be to drop about two drops of oil in each bearing every 100 to 150 miles ridden, and in case the bearings become dirty or gummy, and you have not time to take them apart, fill them with kerosene and let it stand an hour or two; then squirt a quantity of fresh kerosene through the bearings to clean them out.

Wipe as dry as possible and re-oil with fresh lubricant.

The chain should be lubricated with graphite, NOT with oil. This can be procured at any first class cycle agency. Graphite is a black, dry powder, and can be applied with a camel hair brush. A good way to apply it is to keep it in a cheap tin oiler, (sold at cycle agencies for 15 cents,) squirting it out as you would oil. The chain should be kept reasonably clean. When it becomes foul and dirty, so as to run hard, clean it with benzine and a tooth brush.

Never tinker with your machine, or let any but a skilled mechanic repair it if broken or in need of a repairer's attention. It will be cheaper in the end, and more satisfactory, to let a regular cycle repairer make any repairs that may be necessary. In case of breakage of any but a very important part, as a part of the hollow frame, it will only be necessary to buy the part new, when you can put it on yourself with the aid of the wrench furnished with each machine. American machines are all made on the interchangeable plan, and parts to replace those broken, may be ordered from the nearest bicycle agent, and will be found to fit exactly without tool-work or fitting.

Keep all nuts, bolts and screws tight, and the bearings properly adjusted. The bearings will need adjusting only when there is side play. The adjustment should be made so as to take up all side play, and yet leave the bearing so it will turn at the slightest touch.

"Care may have killed the cat, but it never hurt a bicycle. It is everything in the life and satisfaction of running a wheel. Two riders buy a wheel exactly alike at the same time; one cares for his and keeps it systematically oiled, and finds that after he has ridden it ten thousand miles it is in better condition and is worth more than the other man's wheel, which has not had good care, after two thousand miles' use. Look about you and you will see the force of this illustration."

LAW OF THE ROAD.

It is well settled that bicycles and tricycles are carriages within the meaning of the law, and their riders are entitled to the same rights and subject to like duties and liabilities as the riders and drivers of carriages and other like vehicles, and may go upon those parts of the road where other vehicles can, and, on the other hand, should not go where others cannot. Wheelmen have their rights and their duties in travelling upon the highway.

The Statutes of Massachusetts require the cities and towns to keep the roads in repair so that they shall be reasonably safe and convenient for travellers with their horses, teams and carriages at all seasons of the year. (Pub. Sts., Ch. 52, Sec. 1.) Ample provisions are also made to require cities and towns to keep roads in proper condition in accordance with this rule of the Statute.

A road is said to be in repair in accordance with these provisions when the travelled part is without obstruction or structural defects which endanger the safety of the traveller, and properly level and smooth, guarded by railings where necessary, to enable persons by the exercise of ordinary care to travel with safety and convenience. (Dillon on Municipal Corporations, Secs. 103, 112, and Note 3; Hixon vs. Lowell, 13 Gray, 59, 62.)

It also follows that roads are made for the use of travellers with their horses, teams, and carriages, and all such persons are entitled to the lawful occupation of the road, and have the right to pass upon it free from any obstruction.

The highway is established for the convenience of travellers, and the use of it for any game or sport that actually exposes or puts to hazard the personal safety of the traveller thereon is not justifiable, and subjects the party thus using the road improperly to the payment of all damages occasioned thereby to travellers. (Vosburgh vs. Moak, I Cushing, 453.)

It is a grave question whether road races and like uses of the way is not so far improper as to render those engaged in them liable to all damages to travellers which may result.

As regards travellers themselves, each may use it to his own best advantage, but with a just regard to the like rights of others.

Persons in light carriages for the conveyance of persons only, have occasion and of course a right when not expressly limited by law to travel at a high rate of speed so that they do not endanger others. But all foot passengers, including aged persons, women and children, have an equal right to cross the streets, and all drivers of teams and carriages are bound to respect their rights, and regulate their own speed and movements in such a manner as to not violate the rights of such passengers. (Commonwealth vs. Temple, 14 Gray, 69, 75.)

The great and substantial purpose of the law is to afford facilities for the passage of travellers, and the transportation of property over the public highways. All persons may lawfully go and travel over them with any vehicle or animal which is suitable for a way prepared for the purpose of supplying the usual and common accommodation for persons having occasion to pass over the same. (Blodgett vs. Boston, 8 Allen, 237, 239: Gregory vs. Adams, 14 Gray, 242, 247.)

Carriages cannot go upon the sidewalks and parts of the way especially constructed for foot passengers. (Macomber vs. Taunton, 100 Mass., 255.)

The Statutes of the Commonwealth make the following provisions for persons and vehicles meeting and passing each other, upon the road. (Pub. Sts., Ch. 93.)

"Sec. 1. When persons meet each other on a bridge or road, travelling with carriages, wagons, carts, sleds, sleighs, or other vehicles, each person shall reasonably drive his carriage or other vehicle to the right of the middle of the travelled part of the bridge or road, so that their respective carriages or other vehicles may pass each other without interference."

Fred F. Dudley

162-164 Columbus Ave., Boston, Mass.

PREMIER

www.ingramcontent.com/pod-product-compliance
Lightning Source LLC
Chambersburg PA
CBHW032204010726
47493CB00008BA/2815